D0526371

MR. CHATTERBOX'S
Parrot

Original concept by Roger Hargreaves
Illustrated and written by Adam Hargreaves

MR. MEN   LITTLE MISS

MR. MEN™ LITTLE MISS™ © THOIP (a SANRIO company)

Mr Chatterbox's Parrot © 2014 THOIP (a Sanrio company)
Printed and published under licence from Price Stern Sloan, Inc., Los Angeles.
First published in France 1998 by Hachette Livre
This edition published in 2015 by Dean, an imprint of Egmont UK Limited,
The Yellow Building, 1 Nicholas Road, London W11 4AN

ISBN 978 0 6035 7190 9
63570/1
Printed in Great Britain

All rights reserved. No part of this publication may be reproduced, stored in a retrieval system, or transmitted, in any form or by any means, electronic, mechanical, photocopying, recording or otherwise, without the prior permission of the publisher and copyright owner.

Mr Quiet's very quiet house is surrounded by a very quiet garden.

Even the wind doesn't blow there for fear of making a noise in the leaves of the trees.

But one day, a certain someone came to live in the oak tree in Mr Quiet's garden.

Can you guess who it might be?

"Squawk! Wake up! Wake up! I'm a pretty boy! I'm a pretty boy!"

A parrot! A noisy parrot was now Mr Quiet's new neighbour.

The new neighbour that meant the end of all his peace and quiet.

Now, not far away lived Mr Chatterbox. Mr Chatterbox who talks on and on and on, and sometimes on.

"What a good job you are doing," he said to the window cleaner. "Really a very good job, I must say, and in fact I do say, because I have never seen anyone clean windows quite as well as you, in fact, at all as well as you, which is to say …"

From morning 'til night, Mr Chatterbox talks on and on about everything and anything …

… to anyone who will or won't listen!

When the postman delivers the post, Mr Chatterbox talks to him about the rain and the sun and the clouds and the wind and the time, until there is no time for the postman to deliver any more letters.

On and on and on and on.

When Mr Chatterbox meets somebody in the street, it's just the same.

"Good morning, Mr Strong. What interesting things do you have in your basket? Ah eggs, how I love eggs, so tasty with bacon, so tasty boiled or scrambled or fried or baked or coddled or poached. Tell me, how do you like your eggs? Boiled or scrambled or fried or baked or coddled or poached …"

On and on and on and on. What a chatterbox!

It was too much.

Little Miss Bossy called a meeting.

"All those who think Mr Chatterbox talks too much put up your hand!" ordered Little Miss Bossy.

Everyone at the meeting put their hand up. Some put two hands up!

But how could they stop Mr Chatterbox from talking so much? That was the problem.

And nobody had any ideas.

Do you have an idea? If you do, please tell Little Miss Bossy and her friends!

"I may have an idea," said a very small, shy voice. "I have a friend called Mr Quiet who hates any kind of noise and …"

It was Little Miss Shy and she told everyone at the meeting her idea.

Can you guess what her idea might be?

"Hooray for Little Miss Shy," everyone cried. "Hip, hip hooray! Hip, hip hooray!"

Little Miss Shy blushed.

The next day, when Mr Quiet opened his window, he expected to hear the loud squawks of his neighbour the parrot.

But there was complete silence in his garden.

And why was there silence?

Because the parrot was gone.

At last, Mr Quiet had peace and quiet again.

And as for Mr Chatterbox? Well, he was delighted. At last he had found someone who he could talk to as much as he wanted. Whether they were in the car …

… or at home.

And he talked and talked and talked and talked.

On and on and on and on.

And if ever the parrot had had enough of Mr Chatterbox's talking, he would simply fly over and drop a cloth over his head so that, just for a change, he could speak.

"And on! And on! And on!" squawked the parrot!